My Year in
Soccer

A Sports Record Book

WARNER **W** TREASURES™
Published by Warner Books
A Time Warner Company

Warner Treasures is a trademark of Warner Books, Inc.

Warner Books, Inc.
1271 Avenue of the Americas
New York, NY 10020

 A Time Warner Company

Book design by Leandra Jones
Cover design by Lisa C. McGarry

My Year in Soccer is produced by becker&mayer!, Ltd.

Printed in Singapore.
First Printing: March 1996
10 9 8 7 6 5 4 3 2 1

ISBN: 0-446-91133-X

My Year in Soccer

A Sports Record Book

by _____

My Year in Soccer

What better way to keep track of your progress through the upcoming season than by keeping a diary of your team's successes!

All you have to do is carefully observe every game you play in—and after the game is over, take a few moments to fill in the blanks on the pages for that game. Do this after every game and, by the time the season wraps up, you'll have a permanent diary of your year in soccer.

It's easy, fun to do, and best of all, by writing a complete record of your sports season you're writing your own book! And when the season comes to an end, you'll be able to place your diary in a treasured spot on your bookshelf.

Be sure to write your name on the title page of your sports journal. After all, how many kids your age can claim to have written a book?

MY YEAR IN SOCCER

Year: 2001

My name: Jason

My team's name: Jagwires

My coach's name: Mr. Felice

My uniform number: 2

My team's league: 49

My height: 50 inches

My weight: 56 Pls

MY TEAMMATES

Grant

Stefeny

Jamie

Me

Markes

Merin

Branden

Antwone

GAME

Date of game: _____

Our opponent: _____

Where the game was played: _____

Weather conditions: _____

_____

Final score: 6 to 0

Positions I played: forward

_____

Shots on goal: 4

Goals scored: 6

Assists: _____

Shots blocked: 1

Plays I made well: _____

_____

Things I need to work on: _____

_____

What the coach told me
about my performance: Play on
side

Who Really Invented Soccer?

Most sports historians agree that what we know as the game of soccer—by far the most popular sport played in the world today—was first defined by the British in 1863, when the London Football Association wrote the official rules of the sport.

However, the concept of kicking a ball in a competitive manner dates way back. The Chinese emperor Huang-Ti is believed to have invented a similar game, called *tsu-chu*, in 1697 B.C. *Tsu-chu* featured a leather ball that participants kicked with their feet.

The Chinese emperor Huang-Ti invented a game very similar to soccer in 1697 B.C.

GAME

MY SEASON SO FAR

Offense:

Shots on Goal _____

Goals Scored _____

Assists Made _____

Defense:

Steals/Take-Aways _____

Tackles _____

Shots Blocked _____

Overall Play:

Positions Played _____

Headers _____

Throw-Ins _____

Corner Kicks _____

Team Record: _____

How I Would Rate My Play So Far:
(SCORE 1–10: 1-OUTSTANDING; 5-AVERAGE; 10-POOR)

Passing _____

Shooting _____

Defense _____

Dribbling/Ball Control ___

Team Player _____

Gloves for Goalies

Did you ever wonder why so many goalkeepers wear gloves—even when it's hot outside?

As you probably already know, goalies don't wear gloves just to keep their hands warm. Rather, the special lightweight gloves that most goalies wear have rubberized padding. This rubber-like material allows the goalie to get a much better grip on the leather soccer ball—especially when the field and ball are damp.

There's nothing more heart-breaking than to seemingly catch a shot on goal, only to see the slippery leather ball slide through one's hands—and into the goal.

Try on some goalie gloves and then catch a few balls—you'll feel the difference right away.

Goalies wear gloves for a better grip— not to keep their fingers warm.

2
GAME

Date of game: _____

Our opponent: _____

Where the game was played: _____

Weather conditions: _____

_____

Final score: _____

Positions I played: _____

_____

Shots on goal: _____

Goals scored: _____

Assists: _____

Shots blocked: _____

Plays I made well: _____

_____

Things I need to work on: _____

_____

**What the coach told me
about my performance:** _____

_____

The Biggest Upset in World Cup Play

Soccer historians will always disagree about which contest was the biggest upset of all time, but many point to the United States' victory over England in the 1950 World Cup as being the biggest soccer upset of them all.

At the time, the English national team was considered one of the greatest clubs in the world. The American team was nothing more than a rag-tag assembly that hadn't often practiced together.

But lo and behold, they scored the only goal when Joe Gaetens headed the ball past the English goalkeeper. When news services around the world printed that the final score of the game was USA 1, England 0, most soccer fans assumed that it was a typographical error. But no—it was true!

To this day, the incredible United States' World Cup victory over England in 1950 stands as one of the greatest upsets of all time.

2
GAME

MY SEASON SO FAR

• •

Offense:

Shots on Goal _____

Goals Scored _____

Assists Made _____

Defense:

Steals/Take-Aways _____

Tackles _____

Shots Blocked _____

Overall Play:

Positions Played _____

Headers _____

Throw-Ins _____

Corner Kicks _____

Team Record: _____

How I Would Rate My Play So Far:
(SCORE 1–10: 1-OUTSTANDING; 5-AVERAGE; 10-POOR)

Passing _____

Shooting _____

Defense _____

Dribbling/Ball Control ____

Team Player _____

Handball Defined

Although most American sports fans know that a handball is illegal in soccer, they probably don't know that no part of the arm, from armpit to fingernails, can come in contact with the ball.

That is, should you happen to bump the ball with your elbow, forearm, or biceps, it is considered an illegal handball, and the referee will blow his whistle and stop play.

Hey, keep your hands—and armpits— to yourself!

3

GAME

Date of game: _____

Our opponent: _____

Where the game was played: _____

Weather conditions: _____

_____

Final score: _____

Positions I played: _____

_____

Shots on goal: _____

Goals scored: _____

Assists: _____

Shots blocked: _____

Plays I made well: _____

_____

Things I need to work on: _____

_____

**What the coach told me
about my performance:** _____

_____

When is the Ball Out of Bounds?

In basketball, if you step on the boundary line when you have the ball in your hand, you're out of bounds—and the ball is turned over to the other team. In American football, if you step on the sideline while you have the ball, the ref blows his whistle and the play is dead.

For a ball to be in play, a player can be inside or outside the sideline—all that matters is where the ball is.

But in soccer, the ball continues to be in play so long as some part of the ball is still touching the sideline. That is, even though most of the ball is seemingly out of bounds, as long as some part of it remains in contact with the line, you can—and should—continue to play it. It doesn't matter where the player is standing.

3
GAME

MY SEASON SO FAR

● ●

Offense:

Shots on Goal _____

Goals Scored _____

Assists Made _____

Defense:

Steals/Take-Aways _____

Tackles _____

Shots Blocked _____

Overall Play:

Positions Played _____

Headers _____

Throw-Ins _____

Corner Kicks _____

Team Record: _____

How I Would Rate My Play So Far:

(SCORE 1–10: 1-OUTSTANDING; 5-AVERAGE; 10-POOR)

Passing _____

Shooting _____

Defense _____

Dribbling/Ball Control ____

Team Player _____

Proper Soccer Warm-Up

Before you dash out to play, take a few minutes to loosen your leg muscles. Stretch your hamstrings by crossing your legs while standing up straight, and then try to touch your toes. Next, do some groin stretches by spreading your legs apart and leaning first to the right and then to the left.

Finally, get your leg muscles ready for action by jumping back and forth over your soccer ball as quickly as you can. This is an excellent way to get your blood flowing and to warm your body—especially on cold days.

Too many players run out on the soccer field without first taking the time to warm up.

GAME 4

Date of game: _____

Our opponent: _____

Where the game was played: _____

Weather conditions: _____

_____

Final score: _____

Positions I played: _____

_____

Shots on goal: _____

Goals scored: _____

Assists: _____

Shots blocked: _____

Plays I made well: _____

_____

Things I need to work on: _____

_____

What the coach told me
about my performance: _____

_____

How to Run Faster

Surprisingly, while everyone knows how to run, many players don't know that they could run even faster if they learned how to run properly. To build speed, pump your arms forward and backward when you run hard—don't pump them *across* your body. Keep your head up at all times, and get in the habit of lifting your knees and feet as high as you can.

To build even more speed, purchase a pair of leg or ankle weights. Practice with them on, and within a matter of weeks your leg muscles will feel much stronger—and you'll be faster.

Soccer is a running game—primarily sprints of 30 to 40 yards.

4
GAME

MY SEASON SO FAR

Offense:

Shots on Goal _____

Goals Scored _____

Assists Made _____

Defense:

Steals/Take-Aways _____

Tackles _____

Shots Blocked _____

Overall Play:

Positions Played _____

Headers _____

Throw-Ins _____

Corner Kicks _____

Team Record: _____

How I Would Rate My Play So Far:
(SCORE 1–10: 1-OUTSTANDING; 5-AVERAGE; 10-POOR)

Passing _____

Shooting _____

Defense _____

Dribbling/Ball Control _____

Team Player _____

The Throw-In

It's a simple play—throwing the ball back into the game—but remember, always throw the ball with both hands over your head at the same time, and with both feet firmly planted on the ground. No jumping is allowed!

If the referee feels that your throw-in is illegal, he or she will blow the whistle and award the throw-in to the other team.

It's amazing how few new players execute throw-ins properly.

GAME

Date of game: _____

Our opponent: _____

Where the game was played: _____

Weather conditions: _____

_____

Final score: _____

Positions I played: _____

_____

Shots on goal: _____

Goals scored: _____

Assists: _____

Shots blocked: _____

Plays I made well: _____

_____

Things I need to work on: _____

_____

**What the coach told me
about my performance:** _____

_____

Hockey or Soccer—Which is Harder to Defend?

In hockey, the standard goal opening is 6 feet by 4 feet. That's a relatively small area, and it's one reason why there are so few shut-outs in hockey.

In soccer, however, the international standard goal size is 24 feet by 8 feet. If you do a little math, you'll come to the conclusion that a soccer goalie has to guard an area that is eight times larger than that protected by a hockey goalie!

In order for a goal to be counted, the ball must go completely past the goal line.

5
GAME

MY SEASON SO FAR

Offense:

Shots on Goal _____

Goals Scored _____

Assists Made _____

Defense:

Steals/Take-Aways _____

Tackles _____

Shots Blocked _____

Overall Play:

Positions Played _____

Headers _____

Throw-Ins _____

Corner Kicks _____

Team Record: _____

How I Would Rate My Play So Far:
(SCORE 1–10: 1-OUTSTANDING: 5-AVERAGE: 10-POOR)

Passing _____

Shooting _____

Defense _____

Dribbling/Ball Control ____

Team Player _____

Yellow Cards vs. Red Cards

If, in the sole opinion of the referee, a player is particularly violent or rough, is using abusive language, or is totally unsportsmanlike, the referee can stop the game and show the offending player a red card. The player is then immediately ordered from the field of play.

As you might imagine, getting a red card is a very serious offense in a soccer match, but a yellow card is also quite serious.

However, while a red card calls for an immediate ejection, a yellow card serves as an official warning that the player should tone down his or her play. If that same player is shown a yellow card again in the same game, he or she is immediately ordered from the field and thrown out of the game.

Yellow is a warning; red means you're out.

GAME

Date of game: _____

Our opponent: _____

Where the game was played: _____

Weather conditions: _____

_____

Final score: _____

Positions I played: _____

_____

Shots on goal: _____

Goals scored: _____

Assists: _____

Shots blocked: _____

Plays I made well: _____

_____

Things I need to work on: _____

_____

**What the coach told me
about my performance:** _____

_____

Why Do Goalies Wear Funny Shirts?

One of the nice things about soccer is that, unlike most other sports, you don't need much equipment. Besides an inflated soccer ball, all you need is a good pair of soccer shoes, some shin guards, and, if you're the goalie, a shirt distinctly different in color from the other players' shirts.

Why does the goalie need this unusual bit of equipment? Quite simply, so that he or she is easily recognizable to everyone on the field as the goalie. That becomes important when there's a lot of fast-paced action around the goal and it's difficult to keep track of who's who.

The goalie wears a bright shirt to stand out from the other players.

6
GAME

MY SEASON SO FAR

• •

Offense:

Shots on Goal _____

Goals Scored _____

Assists Made _____

Defense:

Steals/Take-Aways _____

Tackles _____

Shots Blocked _____

Overall Play:

Positions Played _____

Headers _____

Throw-Ins _____

Corner Kicks _____

Team Record: _____

How I Would Rate My Play So Far:
(SCORE 1–10: 1-OUTSTANDING; 5-AVERAGE; 10-POOR)

Passing _____

Shooting _____

Defense _____

Dribbling/Ball Control ____

Team Player _____

Dribbling the Ball on Your Foot

One of the best ways to develop the ability to control a soccer ball is by learning how to dribble a ball on either foot. Any experienced soccer player will show you how many times he or she can knock a ball up in the air, over and over again.

The trick to learning this skill is simple: you have to be patient. At first you'll find it quite frustrating. Chances are you won't be able to dribble the ball more than once. Just remember to keep your foot steady and outstretched. Try to relax the top of your foot and catch the ball with each tap. Don't knock the ball too high in the air.

Don't give up! The more you practice dribbling, the more proficient you will become.

GAME

Date of game: _____

Our opponent: _____

Where the game was played: _____

Weather conditions: _____

_____

Final score: _____

Positions I played: _____

_____

Shots on goal: _____

Goals scored: _____

Assists: _____

Shots blocked: _____

Plays I made well: _____

_____

Things I need to work on: _____

_____

**What the coach told me
about my performance:** _____

_____

Develop Your Peripheral Vision

One of the most important aspects of learning how to pass the ball in soccer demands that you have a clear vision of the entire field and all the players on it. To do that you have to be able to dribble the ball without looking down at it.

To strengthen your ability to "feel" the ball without looking down, try this rather novel drill. Stand in one spot with the ball at your feet and have your teammates form a circle around you. Next, blindfold yourself (or just close your eyes) so that you can't see.

Practice passing the ball to individual teammates by listening to their voices. You'll be amazed at how quickly you'll learn to "feel" the ball with your feet, and how good you can become at directing the ball without looking at it.

Experienced players refer to the ability to dribble a ball without looking at it as "having a feel" for the ball.

GAME 7

MY SEASON SO FAR

• •

Offense:

Shots on Goal _____

Goals Scored _____

Assists Made _____

Defense:

Steals/Take-Aways _____

Tackles _____

Shots Blocked _____

Overall Play:

Positions Played _____

Headers _____

Throw-Ins _____

Corner Kicks _____

Team Record: _____

How I Would Rate My Play So Far:
(SCORE 1–10: 1-OUTSTANDING; 5-AVERAGE; 10-POOR)

Passing _____

Shooting _____

Defense _____

Dribbling/Ball Control _____

Team Player _____

Heading a Ball

Some new players are under-standably nervous at the thought of smashing a soccer ball with their head. A well-inflated soccer ball is not exactly soft, and the idea of banging it with one's head can be a little intimidating.

First and foremost, when you head a ball, you want to make contact with the top part of your forehead—not the crown (or top) of your head and, of course, not your face. Most important, when you head the ball, you want to "bull" your neck (tilt your head back a bit), and then hammer at the ball with your forehead.

Practice this technique at home by first using a soft soccer ball or even a balloon. Once you get the hang of it, practice with a regular soccer ball.

One trick to mastering the skill of heading a ball: don't use your face!

8

GAME

Date of game: _____

Our opponent: _____

Where the game was played: _____

Weather conditions: _____

_____

Final score: _____

Positions I played: _____

_____

Shots on goal: _____

Goals scored: _____

Assists: _____

Shots blocked: _____

Plays I made well: _____

_____

Things I need to work on: _____

_____

**What the coach told me
about my performance:** _____

_____

How to Receive the Ball

Even though you can't use your hands to direct a soccer ball's movement, there are numerous ways in which you can receive, stop, and move the ball. To that end, you should become adept at using your head, chest, stomach, thighs, and the inside of your foot to stop a pass that is coming your way.

To practice, have a teammate who's standing no more than six feet away from you roll the ball toward you. Get in the habit of stopping the ball quickly, with the instep of either foot.

Next, have a teammate toss the ball up in the air toward you. Use your chest, stomach, or head to catch the ball, letting it drop to the ground where you can then direct it with your feet.

To direct a soccer ball's movement, you should become adept at using your head—and then some.

8
GAME

MY SEASON SO FAR

Offense:

Shots on Goal _____

Goals Scored _____

Assists Made _____

Defense:

Steals/Take-Aways _____

Tackles _____

Shots Blocked _____

Overall Play:

Positions Played _____

Headers _____

Throw-Ins _____

Corner Kicks _____

Team Record: _____

How I Would Rate My Play So Far:
(SCORE 1–10: 1-OUTSTANDING; 5-AVERAGE; 10-POOR)

Passing _____

Shooting _____

Defense _____

Dribbling/Ball Control ____

Team Player _____

How Much Game Time Do You Spend with the Ball?

Good question. According to a study that was done a few years ago, the amount of time that an individual player is in actual possession, or control, of the ball is surprisingly short.

The study showed that the maximum amount of contact a player had with the ball was just under four minutes out of a ninety-minute game. The least amount of time was only twenty seconds—not much for an entire game.

The average amount of control time was just about two minutes for each player. Again, not much time when you think about it.

Try to make every minute of your possession time in each game count.

GAME

Date of game: _____

Our opponent: _____

Where the game was played: _____

Weather conditions: _____

_____

Final score: _____

Positions I played: _____

_____

Shots on goal: _____

Goals scored: _____

Assists: _____

Shots blocked: _____

Plays I made well: _____

_____

Things I need to work on: _____

_____

**What the coach told me
about my performance:** _____

_____

Dribbling and Faking

As you become more adept at dribbling the ball, you should also begin to work on those skills that make you an even greater offensive weapon. Knowing when to dribble, shoot, pass, and fake a shot is essential.

Because a defender will instinctively freeze a bit when it looks like you're going to shoot, it's particularly helpful to you and your teammates if you can master the ability to fake your shot, and then quickly push a pass to a teammate who's closer to the goal.

Remember, the easy part of the game is kicking the ball into the goal—the tough part is setting up the play so that the goal can be scored.

Expert passing ability is the key to scoring consistently.

9
GAME

MY SEASON SO FAR

Offense:

Shots on Goal _____

Goals Scored _____

Assists Made _____

Defense:

Steals/Take-Aways _____

Tackles _____

Shots Blocked _____

Overall Play:

Positions Played _____

Headers _____

Throw-Ins _____

Corner Kicks _____

Team Record: _____

How I Would Rate My Play So Far:
(SCORE 1–10: 1-OUTSTANDING; 5-AVERAGE; 10-POOR)

Passing _____

Shooting _____

Defense _____

Dribbling/Ball Control _____

Team Player _____

Body Coordination

The more you learn how to dribble the ball, all the while moving your body with various fakes and feints, the more dangerous you'll become. It's a natural instinct for an opposing player to look at your face, head, and arms while you're running with the ball—and not to concentrate on the ball itself.

Likewise, if you're trying to strip your opponent of the ball, learn to look down only at the ball. Don't concentrate on his or her body movements.

Among the common "faking" techniques: 1) A player looks one way while going the other; 2) A player dribbles at half-speed, and then bursts into full speed, still controlling the ball; 3) The player pretends to break in one direction, while planning to go in the other.

Remember— your opponent's body movements are designed to deceive you.

10
GAME

Date of game: _____

Our opponent: _____

Where the game was played: _____

Weather conditions: _____

_____

Final score: _____

Positions I played: _____

_____

Shots on goal: _____

Goals scored: _____

Assists: _____

Shots blocked: _____

Plays I made well: _____

_____

Things I need to work on: _____

_____

What the coach told me
about my performance: _____

_____

Passing Drills

Organize a small pick-up game of no more than six on a side. Playing on a small field, make a rule that no one can take a shot on the goal until three passes have been made among teammates.

While this may be frustrating at first, it will eventually get you and your friends in the habit of always looking for the open player. It will also teach you how to make that perfect pass.

Practice is essential to developing the passing skills that are so important for new players.

10 GAME

MY SEASON SO FAR

Offense:

Shots on Goal _____

Goals Scored _____

Assists Made _____

Defense:

Steals/Take-Aways _____

Tackles _____

Shots Blocked _____

Overall Play:

Positions Played _____

Headers _____

Throw-Ins _____

Corner Kicks _____

Team Record: _____

How I Would Rate My Play So Far:

(SCORE 1-10: 1-OUTSTANDING; 5-AVERAGE; 10-POOR)

Passing _____

Shooting _____

Defense _____

Dribbling/Ball Control _____

Team Player _____

Watch Your Elbows!

As you get more experienced, tackling becomes more a part of the game. And while tackling is a skill that has to be practiced to be perfected, it's very important to make certain your elbows don't smash your opponent.

Too many young soccer players instinctively use their elbows as a way of either pushing or knocking down an opponent. Not only is this a potentially dangerous maneuver, it's also illegal!

Your best bet: learn to use your shoulders when trying to muscle the ball away from your opponent. Keep your elbows close to your side. Otherwise, expect to be called for a foul.

Elbow your way through a play and a referee will ask you to leave the game.

11
GAME

Date of game: _____

Our opponent: _____

Where the game was played: _____

Weather conditions: _____

_____

Final score: _____

Positions I played: _____

_____

Shots on goal: _____

Goals scored: _____

Assists: _____

Shots blocked: _____

Plays I made well: _____

_____

Things I need to work on: _____

_____

**What the coach told me
about my performance:** _____

_____

Penalty Kicks

When a foul is committed against an offensive player within the large rectangular area right in front of the goalie, the ball is placed down for a penalty kick. All players, both offensive and defensive, must clear out of the way while the offensive player takes a clear shot at the goal and only the goalie defends.

If the goalie is successful in blocking the shot, play continues! The ball is in play, and an offensive player can kick the rebounding ball into the net. Likewise, defenders should make every effort to clear the ball out of the zone.

A penalty kick is awarded by the referee when a foul is committed against an offensive player anywhere within the penalty box area.

11
GAME

MY SEASON SO FAR

• •

Offense:

Shots on Goal _____

Goals Scored _____

Assists Made _____

Defense:

Steals/Take-Aways _____

Tackles _____

Shots Blocked _____

Overall Play:

Positions Played _____

Headers _____

Throw-Ins _____

Corner Kicks _____

Team Record: _____

How I Would Rate My Play So Far:
(SCORE 1–10: 1-OUTSTANDING; 5-AVERAGE; 10-POOR)

Passing _____

Shooting _____

Defense _____

Dribbling/Ball Control ____

Team Player _____

Does the Weather Matter?

While playing on a wet or damp field will affect both teams equally, other weather factors can give one team an advantage. If you have the choice, always try to play with the wind at your back. The same with the sun. You always want the natural elements to help your attack rather than hinder it.

The wind can only help downfield passes go farther, especially the goalie kicks. And it's always much easier to move the ball to an open teammate when you don't have to shield your eyes from the sun.

Be aware that wind or bright sun can affect your game.

GAME

Date of game: _____

Our opponent: _____

Where the game was played: _____

Weather conditions: _____

_____

Final score: _____

Positions I played: _____

_____

Shots on goal: _____

Goals scored: _____

Assists: _____

Shots blocked: _____

Plays I made well: _____

_____

Things I need to work on: _____

_____

What the coach told me
about my performance: _____

_____

Practice Your Aim!

It's not enough just to be able to kick the ball hard. As you go up the ranks in soccer, you're going to find yourself playing against excellent goalies.

Thus, you'll need to develop your shooting ability until you can hit certain open spaces, or targets, within the goal. You can practice this skill by simply placing a few soccer balls in front of an open goal, and then doing some "target practice"—shooting at the upper left corner first, then the upper right corner, then the lower left corner, and then the lower right corner.

To become a real expert at shooting, practice your drills by kicking first with your right foot and then with your left foot.

12
GAME

MY SEASON SO FAR

Offense:

Shots on Goal _____

Goals Scored _____

Assists Made _____

Defense:

Steals/Take-Aways _____

Tackles _____

Shots Blocked _____

Overall Play:

Positions Played _____

Headers _____

Throw-Ins _____

Corner Kicks _____

Team Record: _____

How I Would Rate My Play So Far:
(SCORE 1–10: 1-OUTSTANDING; 5-AVERAGE; 10-POOR)

Passing _____

Shooting _____

Defense _____

Dribbling/Ball Control ____

Team Player _____

Your Nutritional Needs During the Game

Common sense dictates that you don't want to eat an entire pizza, or a submarine sandwich, right before a game. Since you're going to be running around a lot, you want to eat something that's not only good for you, but will also give you long-lasting energy.

Carbohydrates are excellent as a pregame meal, as long as you eat about an hour or two before the game. That would include, for the most part, pasta and bread. You should also drink a good amount of fluids as part of your pregame meal, especially if you are playing on a hot day.

During the game, sip some water or sports drinks during the halftime break, but be careful not to gulp down too much liquid.

Candy bars are full of sugar but don't do much to keep your energy up for a game. In fact, they tend to drag you down!

13
GAME

Date of game: _____

Our opponent: _____

Where the game was played: _____

Weather conditions: _____

_____

Final score: _____

Positions I played: _____

_____

Shots on goal: _____

Goals scored: _____

Assists: _____

Shots blocked: _____

Plays I made well: _____

_____

Things I need to work on: _____

_____

**What the coach told me
about my performance:** _____

_____

The Outside-of-Foot Pass

This relatively simple but effective outside-of-foot pass technique should be developed by all young players. Whereas most passes are made by using the inside, or instep, of your foot, this one is made by using the outside of your foot.

To execute the pass properly, lock your ankle with your foot pointed slightly down and in. That way, as the ball comes to you, you can point it in any direction you want, simply by propelling it with the outside of your foot.

Soon you'll find that you can use this technique with either foot. With practice you'll become adept at directing the ball.

The outside-of-foot pass is a great weapon to use when you're dribbling the ball and want to pass while on the run.

13
GAME

MY SEASON SO FAR

● ●

Offense:

Shots on Goal _____

Goals Scored _____

Assists Made _____

Defense:

Steals/Take-Aways _____

Tackles _____

Shots Blocked _____

Overall Play:

Positions Played _____

Headers _____

Throw-Ins _____

Corner Kicks _____

Team Record: _____

How I Would Rate My Play So Far:
(SCORE 1–10: 1-OUTSTANDING; 5-AVERAGE; 10-POOR)

Passing _____

Shooting _____

Defense _____

Dribbling/Ball Control ____

Team Player _____

The Back-Heel Pass

Place the ball behind the heel of your foot and, while looking straight ahead, pass the ball backward to a teammate.

Practice this by working with a teammate who's standing about six feet behind you. Take turns passing the ball back and forth to each other.

When you feel comfortable with your style, try making the pass while you're running. It's a little more complicated, but can be even more effective.

While often overlooked by younger soccer players, the back-heel pass is a technique that's really quite easy to master.

GAME

Date of game: _____

Our opponent: _____

Where the game was played: _____

Weather conditions: _____

_____

Final score: _____

Positions I played: _____

_____

Shots on goal: _____

Goals scored: _____

Assists: _____

Shots blocked: _____

Plays I made well: _____

_____

Things I need to work on: _____

_____

What the coach told me about my performance: _____

_____

Shooting the Ball: The Face Technique

If you want to develop a feel for shooting the ball properly, think of it as a big, round face.

If you kick the ball where the ears would be on that big round face, you know you're going to put a lot of spin on your shot. Likewise, if you kick the ball square on the nose of the face, your shot will go low to the goal.

Finally, if you kick the ball where the mouth would be, your shot is going to rise as it goes toward the goal.

Think of the ball as a face. Kick the ears—spin shot. Nose—keeps it low. Mouth—the ball rises.

14
GAME

MY SEASON SO FAR
• •

Offense:
Shots on Goal _____

Goals Scored _____

Assists Made _____

Defense:
Steals/Take-Aways _____

Tackles _____

Shots Blocked _____

Overall Play:
Positions Played _____

Headers _____

Throw-Ins _____

Corner Kicks _____

Team Record: _____

How I Would Rate My Play So Far:
(SCORE 1–10: 1–OUTSTANDING; 5–AVERAGE; 10–POOR)

Passing _____

Shooting _____

Defense _____

Dribbling/Ball Control ____

Team Player _____

The Infamous Banana Shot

Using the "face" technique, strike the ball where the ears should be—give it a strong kick and a strong follow-through. You'll be amazed at what the ball does! A banana shot spins dramatically, so much so that the ball will seemingly curve away from its intended goal. The best time to implement such a shot is from a corner, where you can get a strong leg behind the kick.

The banana shot is a very dramatic shot—and one that can really make a goalie look foolish.

GAME

Date of game: _____

Our opponent: _____

Where the game was played: _____

Weather conditions: _____

_____

Final score: _____

Positions I played: _____

_____

Shots on goal: _____

Goals scored: _____

Assists: _____

Shots blocked: _____

Plays I made well: _____

_____

Things I need to work on: _____

_____

**What the coach told me
about my performance:** _____

_____

The Chip Shot

A simple maneuver to get the ball over a defender's head, and presumably into the goal, is the chip shot. This move is perfected by kicking very low on the ball, so that you practically lift it over your opponent's head.

Practice it by trying to kick the ball at the precise point where the ground and the ball meet.

If you strike a chip shot properly, the ball will lift almost directly straight up into the air.

15
GAME

MY SEASON SO FAR

●●●●●●●●●●●●●●●●●●●●●●●●●

Offense:

Shots on Goal _____

Goals Scored _____

Assists Made _____

Defense:

Steals/Take-Aways _____

Tackles _____

Shots Blocked _____

Overall Play:

Positions Played _____

Headers _____

Throw-Ins _____

Corner Kicks _____

Team Record: _____

How I Would Rate My Play So Far:
(SCORE 1–10: 1-OUTSTANDING; 5-AVERAGE; 10-POOR)

Passing _____

Shooting _____

Defense _____

Dribbling/Ball Control ____

Team Player _____

What's the Best Line-up?

Should your team have a 4-4-2 (four defenders, four midfielders, and two forwards) lineup? Or how about a 4-3-3 lineup? Or perhaps a 3-5-2?

Obviously, this is a strategy decision that is best made by your head coach. Different teams use different lineups depending upon the strengths and speed of their players.

Once you know what kind of lineup strategy your coach wants to use, it's up to you to figure out how to best play your position—ask your coach for tips.

There's no one best soccer lineup. If there were, everybody would use it.

GAME

Date of game: _____

Our opponent: _____

Where the game was played: _____

Weather conditions: _____

_____

Final score: _____

Positions I played: _____

_____

Shots on goal: _____

Goals scored: _____

Assists: _____

Shots blocked: _____

Plays I made well: _____

_____

Things I need to work on: _____

_____

**What the coach told me
about my performance:** _____

_____

Marking a Player

Marking a player means that you're guarding or defending that player, just as you would in basketball. And the best defense is to make certain your opponent never gets much of a chance to handle the ball.

Always stay between your opponent and the goal. Try to play so close that either he or she can't receive the pass, or must pass the ball immediately after receiving it. Remember not to touch, hold, or grab your opponent. But if you become someone's "shadow" for the day, you'll be doing a great job for your team.

After all, if the player you're marking doesn't have time to handle the ball, your opponent won't be able to score a goal.

To keep your opponent from handling the ball, become his or her "shadow" for the day.

16
GAME

MY SEASON SO FAR

• •

Offense:

Shots on Goal _____

Goals Scored _____

Assists Made _____

Defense:

Steals/Take-Aways _____

Tackles _____

Shots Blocked _____

Overall Play:

Positions Played _____

Headers _____

Throw-Ins _____

Corner Kicks _____

Team Record: _____

How I Would Rate My Play So Far:
(SCORE 1–10: 1-OUTSTANDING; 5-AVERAGE; 10-POOR)

Passing _____

Shooting _____

Defense _____

Dribbling/Ball Control _____

Team Player _____

Learn to Communicate

Good, solid communication between teammates gives the ball handler a chance to visualize where everybody is on the field. Since your teammates can't see behind themselves, it's always a good idea to let your buddies know where you are in relation to them.

Speak up. Don't be afraid to make noise. Let your teammates know what they can't see.

In soccer, as with any team sport, communication is vital to the team's success.

Notes

_____

_____

_____

_____

_____

_____

_____

_____

_____

_____